Nettlepatch Farm

HATTIE THE GOAT

Abigail Pizer

MACMILLAN CHILDREN'S BOOKS

First published 1988 by
MACMILLAN CHILDREN'S BOOKS
A division of Macmillan Publishers Limited
London and Basingstoke
Associated companies throughout the world

British Library Cataloguing in Publication Data
Pizer, Abigail
    Hattie the goat.— (Nettlepatch farm series).
    I. Title   II. Series
    823'.914[J]   PZ7

    ISBN 0-333-44734-4

Printed in Hong Kong

It is summer-time at Nettlepatch Farm.
On the farm live Mr Potter, Mrs Potter and
their little daughter Amy.

All the farm animals are outside in the
sunshine.
The pigs and cows are grazing in the fields.

The ducks are swimming on the pond and
Billingsgate is curled up comfortably on the
wall.

Also enjoying the sunshine is Hattie the Goat.
She is nearly a year old and this is her very
first summer.
The days are long and she spends them
doing what she likes best – eating!

She likes eating grass,

she likes to eat nettles,

and she likes eating bilberries – even the stalks!

Hattie will eat almost anything.

One morning, when Hattie is in the farmyard, she sees Mrs Potter working in the vegetable garden. Then Hattie sees the vegetables – rows and rows of them.

The telephone is ringing in the farmhouse.
Mrs Potter hurries indoors.

Hattie looks at the gate. She looks at the farmhouse. Then she looks at the vegetables. In a moment she is through the gate.

She nibbles at the lettuce. She tries the beans.

She tastes the sweet peas.

But then Mrs Potter comes back.
"What *have* you done, you greedy goat?"
Mrs Potter chases Hattie out of the garden.
Hattie knows she has done wrong.

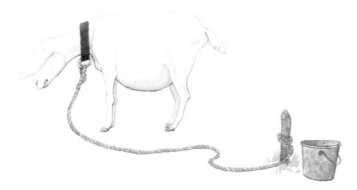

So Hattie is tethered to a post by a rope. Although it is quite a long rope, Hattie does not like it. And she is still hungry. So she tries chewing it. She goes on chewing it and chewing it, until . . .

Quickly, she trots to the gate that led to the
vegetable garden.
It is shut.
Then she sees a line of washing by the
house.

She nibbles at some jeans, she tries a
T-shirt. She tastes some socks. They are

almost as good as the vegetables she ate.
Hattie enjoys Mr Potter's trousers!

Just as she starts on one of Mr Potter's shirts, she hears a shout. Mrs Potter has seen her.
This time Hattie is tethered by a metal chain tied to a stake.

She tries to chew the chain. That's no good. She tries pulling at the chain. She pulls hard – has the stake moved a little?

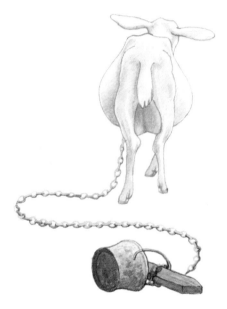

She pulls and pulls and pulls, until – out comes the stake.

She is walking past the big barn when she notices that the doors are open.
Hattie has never been inside the barn. She puts her head round the door for a look.

Inside the barn are bales and bales of hay. More hay than Hattie has ever seen in her life.

Clink, clank goes the bucket, and up climbs Hattie on to the mountain of hay.

Hattie eats and eats. Clink, clank goes the bucket, nibble,
nibble goes Hattie. She eats so much she is quite
uncomfortable – she can hardly stand up.
And then Mr Potter comes into the barn.

Mr Potter is cross.
But he can see that Hattie has eaten more than is good for her.
Hattie feels very sorry for herself.

Hattie is so full she cannot even walk, so Mr Potter picks her up and carries her back to the farmyard.

This time Hattie did not need to be tethered.
She felt so ill that she stayed where she was
put.
Hattie vowed she would never eat again.
Well, not until tomorrow!

Nettlepatch Farm